Lily's Fantastic Dream

Written by Alma Puts Keren

Illustrated by Elisa Rocchi

Collins

Who and what is in this story?

Listen and say

Lily

teddy bear

Download the audio at www.collins.co.uk/839707

monsters

thieves

It is morning. Lily opens her eyes. She had a fantastic dream and she doesn't want to wake up.

I liked my dream!

Lily tells her teddy bear about her dream. She says, "I was a superhero. I went up, up, up in the sky and I was very, very fast!"

"There were bad monsters in my dream.
All of the people in the city were sad.
But I helped the people with my karate.
What a fantastic dream!"

"There was a man with a broken leg in my dream. There was a problem with his wheelchair. I picked him up and flew with him. He was very happy. What a great dream!"

"There were thieves in my dream. They wanted to take some money, but I stopped them. What a great dream! I want that dream again!"

Lily gets dressed and goes to school. She wants to go back to bed. She wants to dream again! She loves her dreams.

Oh dear, no dream!

In the evening, Lily is very tired and goes to bed. She wakes up, but she is very sad. No dream and no superhero!

At school, Lily is sad. She sees a man next to a road, but the cars don't stop for the man.

In her karate lesson, Lily is sad. She thinks about monsters and helping people.

At home, Lily says, "I know! I can read a book about superheroes before I go to sleep. Then I can be a superhero in my dream!"

Lily wakes up in the morning and she is sad. She had a bad dream about school.

So Lily draws a picture of a good dream and puts it under her pillow.

But in the night, she has a bad dream
again. She is sad.

But then Lily thinks, "I don't need to have a dream at night. I can be a superhero in the day!"

So Lily helps people in the city.

"Would you like me to help you?" she asks an old man.

Then Lily helps a shopkeeper in a shop. "There are no thieves. The cat has the teddy bear!" she says.

At school, Lily sees some children push a boy in the playground. She tells her teacher.

That night, Lily is very tired. She goes to bed and she goes to sleep.
Then she has a fantastic dream.

Picture dictionary

Listen and repeat

dream   karate   money   monster

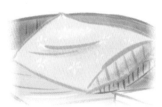  

pillow   push   shopkeeper

superhero   thieves   wheelchair

1 Look and order the story

2 Listen and say

Collins

Published by Collins
An imprint of HarperCollins*Publishers*
Westerhill Road
Bishopbriggs
Glasgow
G64 2QT

William Collins' dream of knowledge for all began with the publication of his first book in 1819.

A self-educated mill worker, he not only enriched millions of lives, but also founded a flourishing publishing house. Today, staying true to this spirit, Collins books are packed with inspiration, innovation and practical expertise. They place you at the centre of a world of possibility and give you exactly what you need to explore it.

© HarperCollins*Publishers* Limited 2020

10 9 8 7 6 5 4 3 2 1

ISBN 978-0-00-839707-4

Collins® and COBUILD® are registered trademarks of HarperCollins*Publishers* Limited

www.collins.co.uk/elt

British Library Cataloguing in Publication Data

A catalogue record for this publication is available from the British Library.

Author: Alma Puts Keren
Illustrator: Elisa Rocchi (Beehive)
Series editor: Rebecca Adlard
Commissioning editor: Fiona Undrill
Publishing manager: Lisa Todd
Product managers: Jennifer Hall and Caroline Green
In-house editor: Alma Puts Keren
Project manager: Emily Hooton
Editor: Frances Amrani
Proofreaders: Natalie Murray and Michael Lamb
Cover designer: Kevin Robbins
Typesetter: 2Hoots Publishing Services Ltd
Audio produced by id audio, London
Reading guide author: Emma Wilkinson
Production controller: Rachel Weaver
Printed and bound by: GPS Group, Slovenia

MIX
Paper from
responsible sources
FSC
www.fsc.org
FSC™ C007454

Download the audio for this book and a reading guide for parents and teachers at www.collins.co.uk/839707